BASEBALL BATS

Sharon Jennings

HIP-JR.

HIP Junior

LIBRARY AND ARCHIVES CANADA CATALOGUING IN PUBLICATION

Jennings, Sharon
    Baseball Bats / Sharon Jennings.

(HIP jr)
ISBN 978-1-926847-12-2

    I. Title. II. Series: HIP jr

PS8569.E563B35 2010   jC813'.54   C2010-906162-4

General editor: Paul Kropp
Text design and typesetting: Laura Brady
Illustrations drawn by: Kalle Malloy
Cover design: Robert Corrigan

1 2 3 4 5 6 7 8 9 10

Printed and bound in Canada

When Mr. Chong is charged with stealing jewelry, Sam and Simon know he isn't guilty. The Bat Gang sets out to catch the real thief but soon the boys get into more trouble than they can handle.

CHAPTER ONE

Where's Mr. Chong?

Last week of school!

One more week and we're out of grade six and out of this school forever!

I high-fived my buddy Simon.

"Ouch!" Simon yelled. "That's my pitching hand, Sam. You want me to pitch a lousy game?"

I rolled my eyes. Simon is a pretty good pitcher, but he acts like his hand is made of glass. Still, our last game was this afternoon. And we were a sure bet to win the championship.

"Sorry," I said. I meant it, too.

The two of us went up the stairs to our old classroom.

"Won't it be great not to see Mr. Chong ever again?" I said. I mean, he's okay, but he's been my teacher three times. First in grade one, then in grade three and now in grade six. With my luck, he'll show up at my new junior high next year.

Simon shrugged. "I like him. And he's a great baseball coach."

Whatever.

We went in the door of our class and Mr. Chong wasn't there. We had a substitute teacher. And not just any sub. It was Mrs. Polk, the mean old lady with the fish-eye stare! The one so ugly we called her Mrs. Puke (behind her back, of course).

"Why are you here?" I shouted.

"Sit down and be quiet," answered Mrs. Puke.

"Yeah, okay, but where is Mr. Chong?"

"SIT DOWN AND BE QUIET!" she repeated.

"Is he sick? What about the baseball game this afternoon?" demanded Simon.

"I ... SAID ... SIT ... DOWN ... AND ... BE ...
QUIET!!!!"

Boy, for an old bag she can really yell. And I
swear she was foaming at the mouth.

So we sat down and shut up. Then Mrs. Puke
began a dumb history lesson. I mean, who cares?

Simon passed me a note. It was written in Bat
code — the secret code we made up way back in
grade three when we started the Bat Gang. Lame, I
know, but we caught lots of bad guys since then.
And we even got our picture in the newspaper a
couple of times!

Uw uvyh it dnof tei uruhw gnihC so. T'nyc ig it
umyg teihtow moh. In hcyic — duofolyeqsod!*

I passed back my note.

Ssucur! Ucoffi!**

Mrs. Puke caught us with the note. She gave us

---

* We have to find out where Chong is. Can't go to game without him.
No coach — disqualified!
** Recess! Office!

6

the fish eye and said she was sending us to the office at recess. The joke's on her because — if you can read Bat code — we were going there anyway!

In the office we had to wait for our school secretary, the world's oldest school secretary. I mean, she must be at least 100 years old. Anyhow, I first asked her, "What happened to Mr. Chong?"

"You're supposed to be outside."

"Yeah, I know, but . . ."

"THEN GO OUTSIDE!" the secretary yelled.

What is it with adults? Why can't they just answer a question without yelling? But then I saw our principal.

"Hey, Mr. Davidson," I called. "Where's Mr. Chong?"

"Sorry, Sam. That's private."

"Is he sick?"

"What about the baseball game today?" Simon added. "We need Mr. Chong to win."

"Sorry about that, boys. But it's just a game."

Just a game? JUST . . . A . . . GAME??

"No it's not," Simon yelled out. "It's the

championship game and it's against St. Jamestown! It's the school that always beats us!" Last year we lost every game to St. Jamestown. Soccer, baseball, hockey, you name it.

Mr. Davidson started to say something and then stopped. I saw a look in his eye and knew Mr. Davidson didn't want to lose again. Not to St. Jamestown.

"Fine," he said. "I'll find someone to coach."

I started to high-five Simon but then remembered his glass hand. We ran outside instead. Funny, we never did tell the office we'd been sent there by Mrs. Puke.

"So what's up with Mr. Chong?" I asked some kid.

The kid shrugged. It turned out that nobody knew.

Then I had a brainstorm. Mr. Chong's kids are in grade one and grade four at this school. We ran to find them and get some answers.

No luck. His kids didn't come to school, either. This was getting really weird. I mean, maybe it was no big deal. Maybe the whole family had flu. But if so — why not tell us?

So, at lunchtime, Simon said, "Let's bike over to Mr. Chong's house. He'll tell us what's going on."

Good idea. Mr. Chong didn't live far away.

So after we ate, we made sure no one was looking (me and Simon are supposed to stay at school over lunch). Then we hopped on our bikes and took off like bats out of . . . whatever. (That's a joke 'cause of our Bat Gang — get it?)

In five minutes we were in front of Mr. Chong's house.

But so were four cop cars and a bunch of reporters!

CHAPTER TWO

On the Case!

Lots of people were out front, just staring at Mr. Chong's house. Cops waved at cars to keep them going and then yelled at all the people blocking the sidewalk.

"Nothing to see! Move along! Move along!"

Of course nobody moved. That just made the cops get madder.

Then all of a sudden people pushed forward. I saw some of the reporters running up the driveway. Cops kept screaming to stay back, but no one cared.

Simon and I leaned our bikes against a fence. Then we hopped up on the seats to get a good look.

What we saw was Mr. Chong coming out of his house with three cops. And he was in handcuffs.

What?!

The officers put Mr. Chong into a police car and left. Slowly people began moving away.

"Beat it! Back to work folks. Show's over," the cops yelled.

Then Simon grabbed my arm and pointed — which made me fall off my bike. He was pointing at Officer Brannon. We knew her from way back and she liked us. "Maybe she'll tell us what's going on," Simon said.

So we pushed our way over and waved at her.

"Sam! Simon! How's it going?" she asked.

"Not good," Simon said. "You arrested our teacher and our baseball coach. What did he do?"

"Your coach? Gosh, I'm sorry. Well . . . it'll be all over the news pretty soon, so I might as well fill you in. You see, Mr. Chong is a suspect in a bunch of robberies. Four jewelry stores were robbed a couple of weeks ago. Lots of things seem to point right at him," Officer Brannon told us.

I was speechless. I mean, no one likes teachers, but Mr. Chong? A thief? No way!

"You're nuts!" Simon said to her. "You've got the wrong guy."

Officer Brannon shrugged. "Well, you two have

solved cases before. Maybe you should ask Mr. Chong to give you a job."

She was joking. Right?

Simon and I ran back to our bikes. We got to school just before the bell. Then we found out Mr. Davidson was going to coach the afternoon game. Mr. Davidson, of all people!

Our new coach sent me and Carla to get our equipment — all new bats, balls and gloves. But I grabbed my favorite old bat, too. Why? Well, d'oh. Like all great players, I have a lucky bat!

Then our team and a lot of the other kids marched the few blocks to St. Jamestown. We sang fight songs and punched our fists in the air. We talked about finally beating St. Jamestown . . . at something. And we talked about Mr. Chong.

We sounded good, but we played a terrible game. No one could do anything right. Simon couldn't pitch, even with his glass hand. And I couldn't hit, even with my lucky bat. Out in the field, no one could catch a ball. At the bases, no one could run without tripping over their feet.

Even Carla, our best base runner, couldn't make it past second.

When it was my turn at bat, I managed to swing and miss — three times. Stupid bat.

"You swing like a girl!" their pitcher yelled at me.

I ran over to the mound. "Oh yeah?" I shouted. But the ump called me off the field.

I threw the stupid baseball bat into some weeds behind the batter's box. Then I sat out the rest of the game on the bench.

Finally it was over. Ten for St. Jamestown, zilch for us.

Of course their team made fun of us. And of course they said some nasty things about Mr. Chong. By now, everyone had heard the bad news. As we left their school, they all sang the "Na-na-na-na Good-bye" song.

Jerks.

Back at our school, the teachers had put together a party. But no one felt like partying.

That night was bad. I ate pizza over at Simon's

and we watched all the news channels. Each one had a story about Mr. Chong. He was charged with four robberies! They kept showing fuzzy clips of a tall, thin man going in and out of jewelry stores. The guy was sort of bald but with a long black ponytail . . . and he sure looked like Mr. Chong. The cops said it was proof that Mr. Chong was checking out the stores before robbing them.

That night our folks felt sorry for us and let us break the rules We slept outside in the Bat clubhouse, even though it was a school night.

And around one in the morning, I had a really good idea. I woke Simon up.

"I've been thinking," I said.

"Uh-oh," Simon mumbled. "That's never good."

"Shut up and listen. We've solved lots of crimes right? But we just sort of stumble into them. I mean, we're not looking for cases. They just sort of come to us, right?"

"Like flies to poop," Simon replied.

"Well, I think this time should be different.

I think we should go after the guy who did this. 'Cause we know it wasn't Mr. Chong. Right?"

"Right," Simon said and fell asleep.

Wrong! Like he said — it's never a good thing when I start thinking.

CHAPTER THREE

The Search Begins!

I woke up the next day and felt lousy. I figured I didn't have to go to school, but my mom figured I did. Guess who won?

The day sucked. Mrs. Puke was awful. Some kids talked trash about Mr. Chong. Me and Simon defended him and so we got into a big fight at recess. Detentions for both of us after school. Then the gym teacher, Mr. Grump, made an announcement about a missing baseball bat. He ordered the whole team down to the gym.

Mr. Grump stood us in a line and went up and down screaming in our faces.

"No sense of responsibility!" he yelled. "You're a bunch of losers! You kids can't even carry your equipment back!" He kept up the shouting and bits of spit flew out of his mouth like a rabid dog. Then he got right in my face and screeched, "What have you got to say for yourself?"

"Man!" I gagged. "Your breath! What did you eat for lunch?"

I guess that's not what he wanted to hear.

Mr. Grump yelled some more. We stopped listening.

"Who cares? It was a crappy bat, anyway," I whispered to Simon

Some kid laughed. "Sure, Sam. Blame the bat."

"Yeah? Well, you couldn't hit anything either, loser!" I said back.

Finally Mr. Grump stopped shouting. Then me and Simon went to the office for our detention.

What a great day. And they wonder why kids hate school.

Still, our folks could see how upset we were about Mr. Chong. Maybe that's why they got us burgers and fries and let us sleep outside in the Bat clubhouse again.

It was about two in the morning when I remembered something. I woke Simon up.

"I've been thinking," I began.

"Again? Wow, Sam! Two nights in a row. You're

going to be brilliant if you keep this up."

I tried to shove Simon out of the Bat clubhouse, but it's up in a tree and that might hurt. Beside, Simon was too fast for me and hung on to a tree branch.

"Okay," he sighed. "What now?"

"I just remembered about that missing bat. I threw it into some weeds when I struck out. It should still be there. Want to go find it?"

"Now? It's two o'clock in the morning?!"

"I can't sleep.

"Boo hoo. Why go look for a dumb baseball bat?"

I smiled. "We could sneak it into the equipment room and then watch Grump freak out when he finds it."

Simon laughed. "Could be funny."

"It *will* be funny," I said.

And so we climbed down from the Bat clubhouse and ran down the street hiding behind trees and bushes as we went. It sure was quiet at 2 AM. No cars. No people. Nothing.

We found the baseball bat right where I said. We found an old ball, too. It looked like some dog's chew toy. So Simon lobbed soft ones at me and I managed to hit one. Then I ran around the field like a madman.

Out in the dark, just me and Simon. No lights. No adults. It was like old times!

Until we heard a car coming along the street. Quickly we dove for cover in a ditch. Simon stuck his head up like a gopher.

"It doesn't have its lights on. And . . . what the . . ."

"What?" I whispered.

Simon slid down beside me. "They're driving onto the field!"

I looked at him and we both scrambled along the ditch as fast as we could, keeping low. We saw some bushes over by the fence and hid. Then we both peered through the branches.

The car stopped right on top off the baseball diamond and two men got out. They both had flashlights and walked back and forth, heads bent.

Then they moved over to the weeds where we had
been five minutes ago. They jumped down and we
could see them searching.

At last they climbed back out, got in the car,
and drove off.

Simon looked at me. "What was all that about?"

I didn't say anything. I just held up the bat and
looked at it.

CHAPTER FOUR

A Brilliant Plan

Had to be! HAD TO BE!! We waited to make sure the car was really gone, and then we raced home. I clutched that bat like it was made of gold.

We pulled the canvas sheets tight around the Bat clubhouse and turned on a flashlight. Then we studied the bat.

"There sure is a lot of duct tape at this end," Simon whispered.

I nodded and began to peel it back. "Someone's

cut out a piece of the handle," I said. "And plugged it back up."

Simon grabbed his Swiss Army knife and dug carefully. Soon he pulled out about an inch of wood. Then he stuck his finger in the hole and pulled out some cotton.

Then he looked at me and I nodded. He held the bat upside down and shook it.

Out they came...

Bracelets. Necklaces. Rings.

Diamonds. Rubies. Gold.

The jewels sparkled in the light.

"Oh man!" I whispered.

"You know what this means?" Simon asked.

"Yeah. That's why I couldn't hit anything yesterday! The balance was off."

Simon punched me. "Moron! These are from the jewelry store robberies!"

"Well duh," I said. "So now what do we do?"

"Go to the police. We have to turn this stuff over."

I nodded, but I was thinking. "What if the cops think Mr. Chong put the jewels in the bat?"

Simon stared at me. "Good point," he said. "No sense getting Mr. Chong into more trouble."

"So let's keep the stuff for a bit. We said we were going to try to prove Chong innocent. Right?"

Simon nodded. "Okay. And we can put the bat back in the gym and see what happens. The real crook will find it and then blow up when he sees the jewels are gone."

"Yeah, but . . . that means we have to be there to see him. We have to catch the crook red-handed. Right?"

"Right," Simon agreed. "So we have to find a way to hide in the equipment room."

But I was still thinking. "I bet it's Grump! Why else did he get so mad about a missing old bat?"

Simon agreed. "So Grump is the real thief but found a way to blame Mr. Chong?"

"It all fits," I said. Then I thought of something else. "But who were those two guys in the car? Grump wasn't one of them. So it must be a gang."

Simon nodded. He didn't say anything, but I could see he was thinking. He does this funny thing where he screws up his face like he has to go potty and then he says something brilliant.

"Sam! The cops are saying Chong robbed four stores. But then this jewelry can't be all of it. There's got to be more hidden somewhere!"

I told you he was brilliant.

Simon kept talking. "We have to sneak into the gym first thing in the morning. We have to look through all the other old bats!"

"What time is it?" I asked.

"Five."

"What if we skip sleeping and just go now? The janitors get there really early to open the school. We can sneak in before anyone shows up."

"What about our parents?" Simon asked.

Darn! Parents always get in the way of a great plan.

But Simon was doing his thinking face again.

"Got it!" he shouted. "We'll both go home and make a mess in the kitchen to look like we've eaten breakfast. Then leave a note to say we went in early. No one will know what time we left."

"Perfect! Now what about the jewels? What do we do with them?"

Simon smiled. "I have a great idea. Remember old Mrs. Hook?"

Of course I remembered her. We thought she was stealing our money and hiding it in her compost bin. It turned out . . . well, if you want to know the whole story, you can look it up. It was in the newspapers four years ago.

"Perfect!" I agreed. I whipped off a sock and we shoved the jewelry inside. Then we snuck over to Simon's backyard compost bin. We took off the lid and gagged. What a smell! I waved the flies away and brushed off the spiders. Then I pushed my sock down deep in all the rotting vegetable junk. No one would find it there.

Quickly I ran down the street to my house. I tiptoed my way around and slopped some milk and cereal in a bowl and on the table and left a note. Then I met up with Simon on the corner. We ran the five blocks to school.

It was still dark and there was no one around.

We hid behind the dumpster bin near the janitor's entrance.

It was damp and smelly, and we saw a couple of fat rats. But even with the gross factor, my stomach started growling.

Then I knew I really *was* a moron.

Why didn't I eat that cereal?!

CHAPTER FIVE

Hiding Places

A janitor arrived and opened the door to the furnace room. Me and Simon snuck in a minute later. It was creepy down in the basement — hardly any light and we could hear mice. But there were places to hide, and we found a good spot behind some leaky pipes. Then we crept down a hallway until we got to the equipment room.

The door was locked.

"Of course it's locked! We're stupid, but the thief isn't!" Simon exclaimed.

Simon looked up at the glass window over the door. It was open just a bit. Then he looked over at the climbing ropes. I figured out what he was thinking.

He ran for a rope and dragged the bottom end over to the door. He held it tight and I shimmied up. I could just reach the window and with a push, it was open. Then I scrambled my way through. Thud! I fell on the floor.

"Find anything?" Simon hissed.

"Yeah! Three more old bats with lots of tape!" I hissed back. Then . . . uh-oh. "Simon! How do I climb up if I'm holding all the bats?"

"You're kidding. Right?" he said.

"No. I'm not kidding. I'm doomed!"

"Open the door, moron."

Oh. Right.

So I opened the door and re-locked and closed it. Then we ran back to our hiding place by the furnace.

Simon pulled out a mini flashlight and peeled back the tape on the bats. Each one had the same

wooden plug! I pulled off my baseball cap as he shook each bat. Just like before, jewels fell out. Soon my cap was full.

I wanted to cheer but then we heard voices. Simon switched off the light and we sat in the dark.

From the talking, we knew it was a couple of janitors. They came real close, but then they left again.

"We've got to get the empty bats back into the gym," Simon whispered. "Then we have to hide and watch."

"What about this stuff?" I asked. I still had a capful of jewels. "Where do we hide it?"

And just then a blinding light shone in our eyes. Somebody grabbed Simon and yanked him out of our spot. I crawled, trying to stay hidden, but the light swept the wall behind me.

"Come out! Now!"

I had just enough time to shove my cap into my knapsack. Then a big beefy arm reached in and grabbed me by my T-shirt.

It was one of the janitors.

"What's going on here?" he yelled. "What are you kids up to?"

My mind went blank. I stood there with my mouth open.

But Simon thought fast. "We were here early. At school. Just playing. And we saw someone sneak in the janitor door. So we followed. Then we heard you and thought you were a thief. Honest."

Wow. Good one.

"A thief? In here?" The janitor let go of my arm and turned, swinging his flashlight into every dark corner.

"Maybe he went off toward the computer room," Simon said.

A brilliant move. In no time, the janitor was racing upstairs.

We grabbed the baseball bats and went back to the equipment room.

"Hey!" yelled Simon. "The door's locked!"

"Of course it's locked. I locked it."

"You *are* a moron!"

Oh. Right.

So I shimmied up the rope again, dropped down into the room, opened the door and let Simon in. Then we stuck the bats back in the box and looked around for a place to hide.

We found it. The space under the stage. We yanked open the double doors. Inside there were the trolleys with the floor mats piled up on them. We could lie on top and be comfy while we waited.

"So the real thief will go into the equipment room and we'll hear him yell when he discovers the jewels are gone. Right?" I asked.

"That's the plan," agreed Simon. "But first, what about the jewels? If we're caught again, we can't have the jewelry with us."

But this time, I was the one with a good idea. "Follow me," I said.

So Simon and I snuck out of the gym and down the hall to the office. I pointed to the fish tank in the corner. It was full of water and lots of colored stones and marbles. There was even a fake treasure chest that gave out bubbles of air.

"Where are the fish?" Simon asked.

"Some kid took them home for the summer," I told him.

I emptied my cap into the tank and all the jewelry sank to the bottom. We reached in and swirled the gravel around until the jewelry looked like part of the set-up.

"Perfect," said Simon.

Just then, we heard a car door slam in the

parking lot. It was 7:30 and teachers were coming to school. We ran back to the gym, yanked open the doors under the stage and lay down on the mats. Then we pulled the doors closed.

"These mats smell," I said. "Like stinky feet."

Simon shone his flashlight around. Lots of cobwebs and candy wrappers and balled up socks and even a pair of dirty underpants.

Gross.

"Tell me again why we're doing this," I said.

"Because we're morons," Simon answered.

CHAPTER SIX

A Thief in the Night

We lay on the mats for a while, bored and hungry. At last we heard the gym door open and we peered out.

Mr. Grump had arrived!

He went into his office and ...

Nothing. No yelling. No swearing. No smashing things.

We saw the gym doors swing wide again and this time it was Mr. Davidson.

"Pete? Pete? You in yet?" he called.

Mr. Grump stuck his head out. "In here. Hey! And guess what? I must be getting old or something. The bats are all here. I don't know how I missed seeing the last one. Now we can donate the whole bunch to that charity of yours."

Huh?

The two of them talked a bit in Mr. Grump's office, then Mr. Grump left and Mr. Davidson was in the equipment office alone. Maybe . . .

Simon looked at me. "Mr. Davidson? He's the crook?"

So we waited and listened but if our principal was the crook, then . . .

Nothing. No yelling. No swearing. No smashing things.

Then Mr. Davidson left, empty-handed. If he was the thief, he would have taken the bats with him. Right?

"Now what?" I asked Simon.

"We stay here and wait. As long as it takes for the thief to show up."

Great.

So we stretched out on the mats and I yawned and Simon yawned and the next thing we knew . . .

We were in the middle of the gym, surrounded by a bunch of little kids. And one angry teacher.

Great. They had pulled the trolley out to use the mats and Simon and I looked like a couple of ugly sleeping beauties.

Of course we got in trouble. In the office we tried to explain.

"Let's hear it," the secretary said, glaring at us. Any 100-year-old secretary has a really mean stare.

"Uh . . . ," I said.

"Um . . . ," Simon said.

The secretary muttered something and sent us into Davidson's office.

"We saw a mouse," Simon told him. "We chased it under the door and then we laid down and then . . . I don't know . . . we sort of . . ."

Mr. Davidson rolled his eyes. "You've missed two periods. Get to class right now."

So we had another bad day with Mrs. Puke and then we went home. My parents were going out

and so Simon and I made hot dogs and went downstairs to watch some TV. But we were so tired, we fell asleep on the couches and never turned the TV on.

And that was a good thing because when I woke up, it was really dark and really quiet. That made it easy to hear the burglar sneaking around upstairs.

"Simon," I whispered. I shook him awake and made the *shhhh* sign. I pointed above me. "Burglar!"

Simon sat right up and both of us listened. Somebody up above was opening closets and cupboards and drawers. Then we heard the squeak of the second step.

We both knew the burglar was heading to the bedrooms upstairs.

It was ten o'clock and my parents weren't home and the house was dark. The burglar thought he was alone!

"This can't just be some random burglar," Simon whispered. "It has to be our guy, and he's looking for the jewels."

"But why did he come here?" I asked.

"He must know you took the bat to the game. He must think you found the loot and kept it."

Made sense.

"And he'll come down here next," I hissed. "We have to hide."

I looked around. There was nowhere. My stomach went into a tight knot.

"Can we get out the basement door?"

So we tip-toed over to the stairs. The door was

just ahead of us, but it was old and made a real *squawk* when you pulled it.

"When I yank it, we have to run. Don't wait," I said.

"Yeah, like I'm going to wait and say hello. We'll run to my house and tell my parents."

"No! We have to see who it is," I argued.

And just then we heard the staircase upstairs creak. We knew the burglar was on his way down.

I turned the knob and tried to open the door quietly, but no such luck. It made a noise like fingernails on a chalkboard. So we shoved it hard and the two of us were outside and down the driveway and across the road in seconds. We hid in the bushes and watched.

Of course the burglar heard us. What would he do? We waited and waited and then we saw a black shadow slip out of the side door. The guy looked back at the house.

It was someone tall and thin. All we could really see from across the street was that the guy had a long black ponytail.

CHAPTER SEVEN

Kidnapped!

Huh? Mr. Chong?!

"But he's in jail!" Simon said. "So we were right! Someone is pretending to be him!"

I nodded, but I didn't take my eyes off the burglar.

The guy ran up the street and got in the passenger door of a car. The car started moving slowly towards us. Then it suddenly stopped in front of my house. The doors were flung wide and two men jumped out.

They came right at us.

Of course! The driver of the getaway car had seen us hide!

Simon and I tried to get out of the bushes. We scrambled like crazy, but it was too late.

Both men were wearing ski masks. The driver was huge and easily grabbed hold of me. The thin burglar had already caught Simon. They clamped their hands over our mouths. I tried fighting, but the one guy twisted my arm behind my back. The pain was so bad I thought I was going to pass out.

Back at the car, they shoved gags into our mouths and tied our hands. Then they popped the trunk and threw us in.

"Not a sound. Get it? One noise and you're done."

They slammed the trunk shut and in seconds we were moving.

In about ten minutes, the car stopped. The trunk opened and the men yanked us out. We were in a deserted parking lot.

"Tell us where you hid the jewelry and we'll let you go."

I looked at Simon and he nodded. We had to tell them or else . . . Well, at the moment I didn't want to think about "or else." Then the big guy grabbed Simon's hand, and I heard something snap. I saw Simon's eyes widen and I saw the pain on his face.

"Talk." He pulled the gag out of my mouth.

"At . . . at sc . . . schoo . . . school," I stammered.

He twisted my arm. "They're not in the baseball bats. Don't lie."

I shook my head, moaning. "We hid them."

He shoved the gag back in my mouth and pushed us into the trunk. They slammed the lid and off we went.

Simon and I lay in the dark, our bodies bumping and banging up against tools and a tire. I wondered if Simon was as scared as I was. We'd been in some tough spots over the years, but this one was starting to look pretty bad. Then the car stopped and once again the men opened the trunk.

They pulled us out and we walked without a struggle. We ended up at the back of the school and my burglar took out a key and opened a door.

I looked at Simon, and I could tell he was thinking what I was thinking. Where did they get a key to the school?

Inside, the burglar pulled my gag out again. It tore at my mouth and I tasted blood.

"Where are they?"

"I'll . . . I'll show you."

"Don't try anything funny or your buddy here will have a broken arm."

They followed me down the hall and around the corner. I stopped at the fish tank. "In there."

The big man leaned in and looked. "You're lying." I saw him reach for Simon's arm.

"No! Wait! They're hidden. With the stones and marbles! You can't see them. Untie my hands so I can show you." Then I reached in, way down, and grabbed two handfuls of stones. I showed them the diamond ring in my hand. "See? All the jewelry is there. Honest!"

They peered in over the side, and I turned to stare at Simon. Then I looked over at the wall and he followed my eyes. He saw the fire alarm and smiled.

The crooks were reaching over the side of the tank to grab some jewels.

I nodded at Simon.

At the exact second he pulled the alarm, I grabbed onto the fish tank with both hands. I leaned into it with all my weight and yanked. The fish tank toppled over and all of us went down in a flood of water and gravel.

So did I, but I knew it was coming. I managed to get to my feet really fast.

Simon and I tore down the hall and out the side door . . . and that set off the regular alarm.

Once we got outside, we could see fire trucks and police cars come tearing up the road.

CHAPTER EIGHT

Proven Guilty!

But not soon enough!

We watched, helpless, as the thieves got into their car. They drove across the playground and baseball field, then smashed through the fence at the other end.

"Did you get the license number?" I yelled.

Simon shook his head, and I saw the pain in his eyes. That's when I untied the gag over his mouth.

"Come on. Let's go tell the cops what happened," I said.

We hurried around to the front of the school. Someone shouted at us to get back but we ignored him. Then cops and firefighters were all around us.

At first they yelled, but that stopped quick. As soon as they saw Simon's hands tied up, they just stared.

"There's no fire!" I shouted. "It was us. We pulled the alarm."

"My hand," Simon sobbed. A cop untied the ropes and a firefighter took a look at Simon's hand.

"What kind of a prank is this?" the cop asked.

I shook my head. "It's not a prank." And I explained as best I could. A police officer phoned Simon's parents. Then another cop took Simon to the hospital. I took the police inside the school and showed them the broken fish tank. There was still jewelry lying on the floor.

"I think the thieves got some of it," I said. "I'm sure there was more." Then I showed them the hollowed-out bats in the gym.

Meanwhile, other cops found the broken fence where the getaway car got away.

So, for once, the cops believed me and didn't think I was the crook. But...

"Why didn't you tell us about the jewels?!"

"Why did you think you could solve a robbery?!"

"Are you a moron?!"

Finally I was able to say something. "Because you think Mr. Chong is guilty. We know he's not because, well, because." I had to pause. "But we needed proof."

And then it dawned on me. We didn't have proof. We had found most of the jewelry that was stolen. And a tall, thin man with a ponytail did kidnap me and Simon. And by hiding the jewelry in the school, it looked like Mr. Chong hid it himself. School was a place he could get into without any trouble.

We made Mr. Chong look even more guilty!

I felt horrible. I couldn't feel any worse. Wait! Not true. It could get worse . . . when my parents showed up.

Blah, blah, blah, was all I heard. It was all the stuff they say when me and Simon get involved with crooks. Snore.

Then I remembered something. "Wait a minute!" I shouted, interrupting my dad. "The burglar can't be Mr. Chong. Mr. Chong's in jail!"

A cop shook his head. "He's been out on bail since last night. Someone's just gone to arrest him again."

Oops.

My parents took me home, and I had a bad night. I couldn't sleep, I was so worried about Simon. Oh yeah — and Mr. Chong.

The next day, Simon was at my door, his hand in a cast.

"Two bones broken," he said. "At least it's not my pitching hand."

"Yeah, but it's not your writing hand either. You can still do schoolwork."

"Tomorrow is the last day of school. I'm not doing anything. I'm just going to school to show off my cast."

But back in class, old Mrs. Puke had other ideas. She made Simon do lots of work even with one hand in a cast. Where's the fairness?!

At the end of the day, Mr. Davidson stuck his head into our room. He asked Simon and me to come down to the office. Now what?

But everything was cool. It turned out that the 100-year-old secretary was retiring and they were having a party for her.

"You've invited us?" I asked. "Nice. Where's the cake?"

"No, Sam," Mr. Davidson said, rolling his eyes. "I thought with all the trouble you've caused around here, you could help out."

Trouble? Great. We almost die and now we're being punished.

"First, please carry these boxes out to Mrs. Wood's car."

"Who is Mrs. Wood?"

Mr. Davidson stared at me. "The secretary! She's been here for twenty-five years!"

Who knew? Mrs. Wood must have spent a quarter of her life at our school.

So we followed Mrs. Wood out to her car. I carried everything because of Simon's broken hand. Mrs. Wood popped the trunk and went back into the building while I tossed the boxes in.

Simon suddenly reached inside with his good hand and pushed the boxes around a bit. I saw his body jerk.

"What is it?" I asked.

When he pulled out his hand, he was holding a wig. A wig with a long black ponytail!

CHAPTER NINE

Caught!

hen I saw a photo in one of the boxes. There was Mrs. Wood standing between two young men. One was tall and thin, the other was tall and huge. The frame said "Family Forever."

"Mrs. Wood?" Simon said. He looked stunned.

I grabbed the photo and slammed the trunk shut. "We have to go to the cops. Right now!"

We looked around but Mrs. Wood was nowhere in sight. I shoved the photo in my backpack, and we ran over to our bikes. Five minutes later we were at the station and talking to Officer Brannon. We showed her the wig and the photo.

She looked at us in amazement. Then she sat back in her chair and laughed. "How you two do it, I'll never know!"

A second later, she jumped up and ran outside to her squad car. We were *not* going to be left behind this time. So me and Simon chased after her and climbed into the back seat. Officer Brannon called for back up and soon we were zooming along the streets, sirens blaring.

"Cool," I said.

And to make a long story short, Officer Brannon arrested Mrs. Wood's two sons. They were sitting at home watching a baseball game on TV. And they were so dumb, there was a big pile of stolen jewelry on the coffee table.

But where was Mrs. Wood? Other cops had gone to the school but she wasn't there.

"She probably saw all the cops outside her house and took off," Simon suggested.

Anyway, even without Mrs. Wood, they let Mr.

Chong out of jail.

"Hey!" said Simon. "Maybe he'll be back at school tomorrow for the last day!"

And that night, our parents let us have a pizza and sleep outside in the Bat clubhouse again. I mean, we had solved a crime, so I guess we deserved it.

Anyhow, Simon and I were just getting sleepy when we heard it. The noise was a snarl and a hiss and a choked-off meow. We looked out and saw Mrs. Wood standing at the bottom of the ladder. She was holding up Simon's cat. And she was squeezing the cat's throat.

"Get down here. Don't make a sound or Fluffy gets it!" the old lady hissed.

"Her name's not Fluffy," Simon said.

"I don't care if her name's King Kong. Get down!"

We jumped from the perch.

"Where are they? Where are the rest of the jewels?"

"But . . . " Then I felt stunned. I looked at

Simon and knew he felt the same. We had totally forgotten about the first batch of jewelry!

"Hurry up!" Mrs. Wood growled. "I know you've got them. I know exactly how much I stole."

Then she shook the cat at us. Simon's cat whimpered, so we had no choice. We led Mrs. Wood to the compost bin at the back of the yard.

"It's in there," I said.

"Get it."

"But it's yucky!" I protested.

"I'm warning you, Sam. I've had enough of you over the years. Move!" She shook the cat again, and it let out a tiny meow.

I took the lid off the bin and reached my hand down. I felt all the gross scraps of rotting food and thought I'd throw up the pizza I'd eaten for dinner.

But then, I had an idea.

"I can't feel it," I said. "I'll have to scoop some out." So I pulled up handful after handful of rotting, slimy garbage. I put all of it on the lid. Mrs. Wood came closer to watch.

Then I bent down one more time and grabbed

the lid. I turned and flung all the compost in Mrs. Woods' face. She let go of the cat and screamed.

Then Simon ran at her and pushed her down. We both started yelling.

"Help! Help!"

MEOW! MEOW! Simon's cat jumped on Mrs. Wood and hissed.

Lights came on all over the place.

But the strangest thing of all came next: Simon's backyard was suddenly filled with cops.

"We've been watching you all night," Officer Brannon told us. "We were sure she'd come after you."

"Really? How come?" I asked.

"Her sons told us some jewelry was missing. Mrs. Wood thought you had stolen it. It made sense she'd follow you."

Mrs. Wood was in handcuffs and the cops were taking her away.

"Wait!" I yelled, and ran over to her. "Why? Why did you do it?"

"Why? You want to know why?" Her eyes were

blazing. "Because I HATE my job! I HATE kids!! I HATE teachers!!! I HATE school!!!!"

I guess it's enough to make you rob jewelry stores.

CHAPTER TEN

Freedom?

L ast day of school!

Mr. Chong was back in class. For once he was happy to see us.

Everyone wanted to hear all about the case. We were heroes!

Then we found out why the police blamed Mr. Chong. It all started because Mr. Chong wanted to buy his wife some jewelry for her birthday. He went to a bunch of stores looking for the right gift. He told Mrs. Wood all about it, even asking her advice. She told her sons and they came up with a plan. Mrs. Wood thought it was funny to lay the blame on poor old Mr. Chong, so her sons robbed the stores he had gone to. One of them wore the wig. The police found her sons had robbed lots of stores before and were already wanted by the police. It turned out they had other stolen stuff buried in their backyard.

"But why hide the stuff in baseball bats?" Simon asked.

"Because Mr. Chong is the baseball coach, moron," I told him. And it felt good that I wasn't the moron for a change.

But Officer Brannon told us more. "She hated Mr. Chong so much she wanted him to go to jail. Mrs. Wood planned to 'discover' the hidden jewelry herself and then call us."

How about that?

The rest you know, except this.

Simon and I got a reward . . . but Mr. Davidson took half to replace the fish tank.

The jewelry stores got together and gave Mrs.

Chong a really nice necklace.

And one more thing. Mr. Chong handed out our report cards. I got a bunch of C's and one A — in gym. Simon got all A's. Big surprise.

At the bottom of my report was a note. It was written in bat code! How did Mr. Chong figure out our code?!

Here's what it said.

Uus eia no Rubmutpus. M'o gnohctows sliihcs dny llow ub reia udyrg nuvus ruhcyut!*

---

* See you in September. I'm switching schools and will be your grade seven teacher!

68

Sharon Jennings is the author of more than thirty books for young people. She began by writing picture books for young readers and later she created novels for the Franklin series of books. For High Interest Publishing she has written *Dancing on the Edge* for the HIP Edge series and *Pump!* for the HIP Jr. series, as well as six Bats mystery novels.

The six Bats novels follow Sam and Simon as they solve mysteries from the first day of school to the last. In calendar order, the books are *Bats Past Midnight*, *Bats in the Graveyard*, *Jingle Bats*, *Batnapped*, *Bats on Break* and *Baseball Bats*.

Sharon says, "There is nothing I like to do more than write. I become the characters and live inside their story." Sharon Jennings lives in Toronto but often visits schools across Canada and the United States. For more information, visit her website at <www.sharonjennings.ca>.

For more information on HIP novels:
High Interest Publishing – Publishers of H·I·P Books
www.hip-books.com